Oct 17

ABOUT THIS BOOK

This book was edited by Megan Tingley and Andrea Spooner and designed by Saho Fujii. The production was supervised by Erika Schwartz, and the production editor was Jen Graham. The illustrations for this book were done in acrylic, pencil, pastel, and ink on plywood, and digitally finished. The text was set in Nicolas Cochin Regular, and the display type was set in Adobe Caslon Bold Italic Swash and Mrs Eaves Bold, traced over with a pencil and then digitally tweaked.

SHINE!

Story by Patrick McDonnell

Art by Naoko Stoop

Megan Tingley Books
Little, Brown and Company
New York Boston

Little Hoshi was a star,

a sea star who lived in the ocean.

Every night she would gaze at the twinkling stars
in the sky above and make a wish.
"I wish I were there instead of here...
Up there, where all is fine. Up there, where I would shine!
Oh, poor little me...a star stuck in the sea."

As the sun rose and the stars disappeared,
the tide swept Little Hoshi back into the water.

"I should be floating among the colorful planets,"
Hoshi thought, as she floated among the colorful coral.

"Imagine all the unique and wonderful friends you could meet up there!" she told her unique and wonderful neighbors.

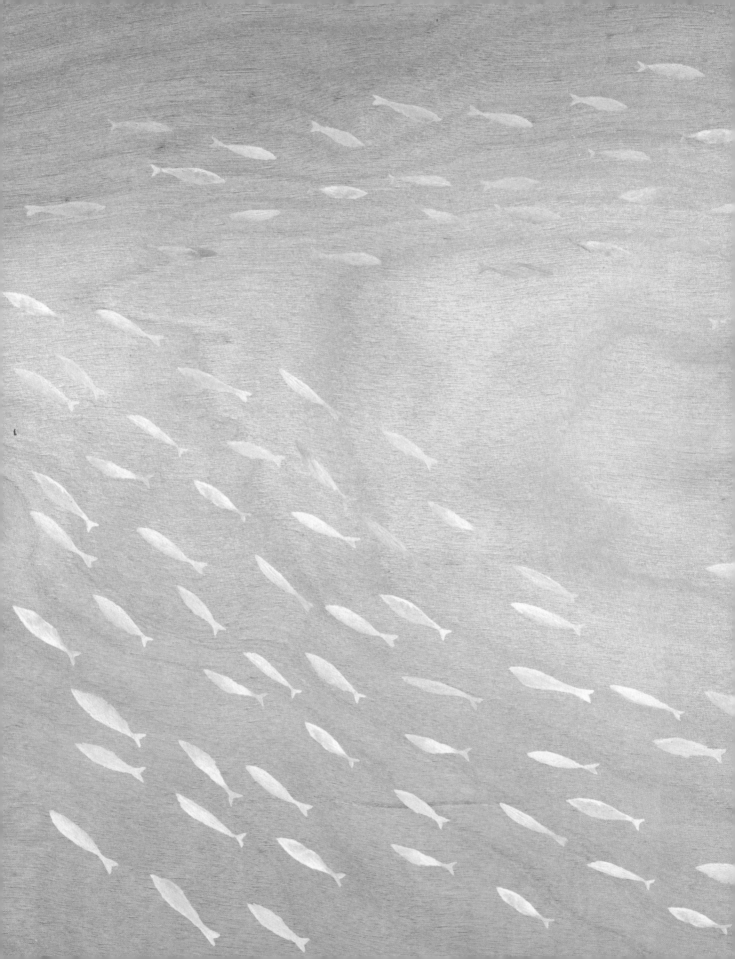

"Up there, there are exciting and endless possibilities,"
she explained to the exciting, endless schools of minnows.

"Where could you see something so magnificent down here?" she wondered aloud to the magnificent blue whale.

"I want to shine!" cried Little Hoshi.

"I wish I were there instead of here.
Down here, nothing is fine. Down here, I'll never shine!
Oh, poor little me...a star stuck in the sea."

Everyone tried to cheer her up.
But she turned and swam far away…
down,
    down,
        down into the deepest waters,
            where she floated to the
                murky
                 bottom.

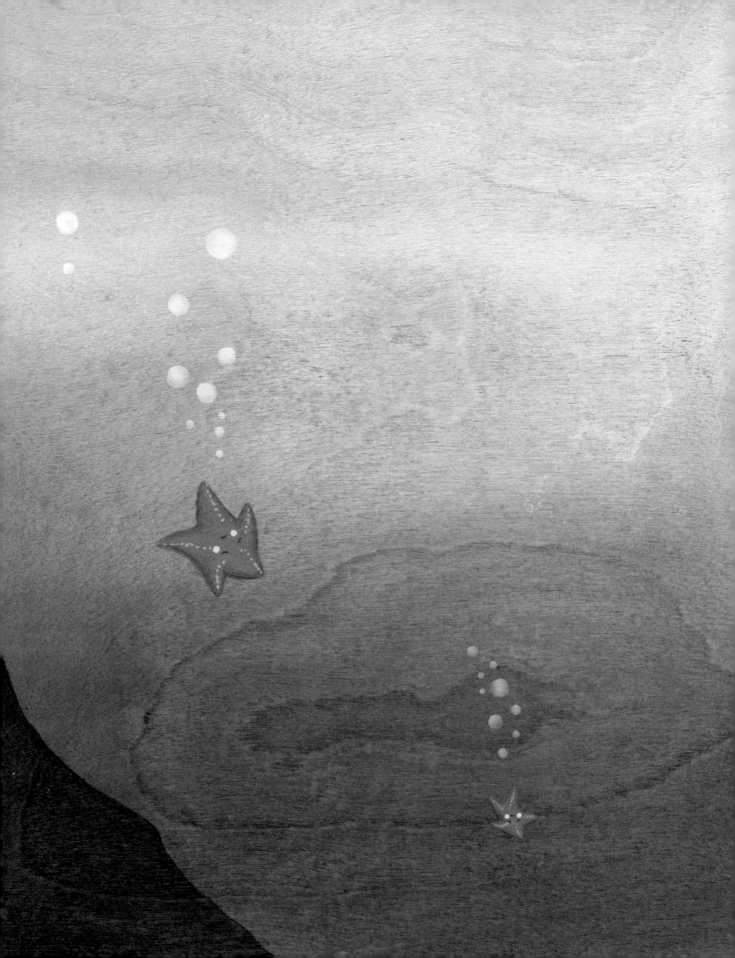

Little Hoshi gazed out into the darkness…
until she saw

A STAR.

She closed her eyes and made her wish.

The star came closer,

closer...

and CLOSER.

But it wasn't a star at all.

It was an anglerfish, with her glowing light.

"Why are you here and not up there?"
the anglerfish asked the little sea star.

"That's what I want to know," replied Hoshi.

"Oh, could you, *would* you, tell me how you shine?"

"It's my pleasure," said the anglerfish.
"I shine because I'm happy. Happy to be here,
happy to be there…happy to be anywhere!
Because happiness, my dear, is always found right…
HERE."

And the anglerfish pointed to her heart and shined.

And all her deep-sea mates joined in.
"Ooowee!" said Little Hoshi. "Thank you!"

up...

up,

And she swam up,

Where everyone welcomed her home.
She gazed at her colorful, magnificent world
and her unique and wonderful friends.
And for the first time, she saw so many exciting
and endless possibilities.

Then Little Hoshi looked into her happy heart…

and SHINED.